TAMANY,

DON'T EAT TURTLE SOUP!

ENJOY,

MARA UMAN HIXON

2010

P.S. HAPPY FIRST BIRTHDAY!

Happy 1st Birthday Tamany! *

Love Always,

Aunt Liana + Uncle Scott

Turtles' Way:
Loggy, Greeny & Leather

Canmore Press, P.O. Box 510794, Melbourne Beach, FL 32951-0794
© 2004 Mara Uman Hixon

First edition 2005

Printed in China on archival paper; library binding.

10   09   08   07   6   5   4   3

Illustrations by Steve J. Harris, owned by Mara Uman Hixon © 2004; adapted by Lyn Cope for design/offset printing 2005.

Cover design by Mara Uman Hixon, executed by Lyn Cope.

Wynden Imprint, Canmore Press children's book, content design by Canmore Press.

The manuscript content was set in Adobe Jenson Pro and ChildsPlay. Decorative elements are Kids and Zeal.

Turtles' Way: Loggy, Greeny & Leather scientifically depicts the life-cycles of Atlantic sea turtles as observed by the author and as explained to her pre-school daughter from their window on the Atlantic Ocean. Depictions of the moon in this book are of crescent moons and full moons because this works artistically. Turtle eggs are laid throughout the lunar cycle and hatch during a similar moon-cycle approximately sixty days after they are laid, as stated in the text. Eggs laid during a quarter moon, hatch in a quarter moon cycle, not during a full moon as rendered in the illustrations.

Dedication

To my father who introduced me to the beach and shared his love of turtles with me when I was a little girl, and to my mother who taught me empathy for all animals.

To Jose, my husband, for being unbelievably supportive, my best friend, and lifelong surfing partner: I love you.

To our beloved daughter, Isabella, to whom I have told this story many times, as we waited for and watched the huge turtles crawl out of the sea, and later as we watched their hatchlings climb from their holes and race toward the waves.

A percentage of the profits are donated to the Sea Turtle Preservation Society.

Wynden *Books*
an imprint of **Canmore Press**
www.canmorepress.com; booksales@canmorepress.com

ISBN 978-1887774-20-8 Library Binding   ISBN 978-1-887774-22-2 Paperback
US $16.95   Canada $18.50   US $9.95   Canada $11.25

Turtles' Way: Loggy, Greeny & Leather

Story by

Mara Uman Hixon

Pictures by

Steve J. Harris

On a warm summer night, three mommy turtles crawled out of the bubbly blue ocean to lay some eggs.
These eggs were going to be their babies one day. The moon was very bright and lit up the sky.
This made it easy for the mommy turtles to see.

1

The first mommy turtle to come out of the ocean was Loggy. She was a loggerhead turtle. Loggerhead turtles have very big heads and very large jaws. Why? Well, because they eat shellfish and use their powerful jaws to break the hard shells — yummy!

The second mommy turtle to emerge from the water was Greeny. She was a green turtle. She had a much smaller head than Loggy. Greeny ate different foods than her friends. She liked to eat sea grasses and algae. This food made her turn green! Silly! But, true.

The last mommy turtle to come out of the sea was extremely slow. Her name was Leather. She was huge! In fact, she weighed over 1200 pounds. Wow! She was almost as big as a car, but not as fast! Leather liked to eat a lot of jellyfish. Her shell was not hard, but it was leathery—kind of like a rubber-band.

4

Loggy, Greeny, and Leather moved ever so slowly up the beach towards the grasses and sea oats. They were each looking for a safe place to lay their eggs that would become their baby sea turtles one day—actually, in about sixty days!

Each mother turtle would stop every so often and stick her snout into the sand and smell it.

Do you know why?
This helped the mommies pick the perfect sand
—not too hard,
—not too soft,
—not too wet,
—and not too dry.

It had to be perfect so their babies could grow in their eggs safely.
Each mommy picked a perfect spot.

5

First, Loggy found her perfect spot. She was very happy. She dug a big hole in the sand with her flippers. It took a long time and was hard work for her. Then, when the hole was dug, Loggy laid her eggs very, very carefully. She had to be very gentle because she didn't want to hurt her babies! Turtle egg shells are flexible so they do not break easily. Thank goodness!

Then, Loggy whispered to her eggs, "I love you, my babies, be safe." Finally, she covered all her eggs with sand to keep them warm and snuggly while the baby turtles grew inside their shells.

Next, Greeny found a fabulous spot. It had really soft sand and was next to an old log on the beach. She dug her hole. Digging it took a long, long time. Her flippers got tired! But, she kept digging. She would do anything for her babies, just like any good mommy would. She also carefully laid her eggs.

Once she had laid all of her eggs, she quietly said,
    "Babies, I love all of you the most. You will all be different and special in your own way. Take care! I love you."

Then Greeny covered her eggs with the soft, white sand. She also made sure all of her eggs were warm and snuggly.

Finally, Leather had to find a spot. She moved slowly because she was so large. But, you know, sometimes the best things take the longest. Anyway, Leather finally found a very nice spot. It was next to the sea oats, under a big sea grape tree. She took an extra long time to dig her hole. She grunted a little bit because it was a lot of work.

As you know, sometimes the hardest things to achieve are the most rewarding. Then Leather laid her eggs. She used her rear flippers to pack the sand over her eggs. She wanted them to be warm and snuggly, too.

She softly told them, "I love you all more than you will ever know—be safe." She turned around and headed toward the ocean.

8

Loggy and Greeny waited for Leather. They called out and asked if she was ready to go.

She said, "Yes, let's go home."

She already missed the warm ocean.

All three turtles turned towards the waves.

They crawled slowly because they were very tired.

9

The turtles kept wiping their eyes with their flippers because tears kept falling. It looked like they were crying, but they were not!

I bet you didn't know that turtles get rid of the extra salt in their bodies through the glands in their eyes. You know, the ocean is very salty. So, even though it looked like they were crying, they really were not.

The three mommies were all salty, sandy, and happy.

Loggy and Greeny kept bugging Leather to hurry up. They wanted to get back home into the ocean. Once they were near the water's edge, they each paused to take a breath, and asked the moon,

"Moon, will you please watch over all of our eggs?"

The moon replied,
"Yes, and I will guide your babies to the ocean when they hatch."

The three turtles felt relieved and crawled faster toward their home. They waded into the water's edge, then dived under the first wave. It felt good to be home again after a hard night's work. It felt good to wash the sand off their flippers.

11

For the next sixty nights, the moon watched over the mommies' eggs. The moon had a hard job. Sometimes, the raccoons would come out of the sea oats to try to dig up the baby eggs. Raccoons like to eat baby turtle eggs. Yuck!

Sometimes, other creatures such as crabs, ants, foxes, coyotes, vultures, dogs, and armadillos tried to eat the little eggs, too.

12

The moon was very busy watching after all
the eggs! The moon worked so hard that each
morning it had to take a break.
Guess what? The sun took over! The sun kept the
eggs warm because it made the sand hot.

Did you know that the eggs in the warmer
layers of sand turn into girl turtles and the eggs in the
cooler layers of sand turn into boy turtles?
Weird, huh? But, true.
The sun watched over the eggs all day long.

13

On cloudy days, the sun would peak out from behind the clouds and check that all the baby eggs were safe. So, even though the mommy turtles were back in the ocean far, far away, the moon and sun were watching over the baby eggs.

The moon and sun were nature's baby-sitters.

14

Two times since the mommy turtles had laid their eggs, the moon had become a tiny sliver and grown big and fat again. At sunset, sixty nights and sixty days later—give or take a few—the moon decided it was time for the baby turtles to hatch from their eggs.

The moon was full, and round, and huge as it climbed up in the sky and over the beach.

It had prepared for the hatchlings by lighting up the whole sky and making a moonbeam path on the beach toward the ocean.

15

The moon called out to all the eggs,
"Dear baby turtles, you must hatch from your eggs
and crawl as fast as you can to the ocean.
Please, baby turtles, follow my light to the ocean.
There are many animals that would like to eat you so,
be careful and crawl quickly!"

16

The baby turtles listened and did exactly what the moon said.
They were not allowed to play just yet. This was serious business!
The babies pecked out of their shells,
dug up through the sand,
popped out of their holes,
and crawled as fast as they could.

The sun was coming up so the moon could rest.

17

Unfortunately, when the sun came up, the birds woke up and started to fly around in search of food. Some birds caught baby turtles and ate them for breakfast — YUCK.

Some turtles got lost and went the wrong way. Raccoons ate them — BLAH!

Poor turtles. But, you know, that is a part of nature's way.

There is an old saying, "Safety in Numbers." As the turtles tumbled out of their nests, they raced toward the ocean. Many of them made it safely to the water's edge!

The baby turtles slid into the ocean. The water was salty and warm. It felt good.
Swimming was fun! The baby turtles caught the currents that helped pull them to their new home, the big blue ocean.

For the first few days, the baby turtles did not have to worry about food, because the leftover yolk from their eggs was in their tummies. The yolk kept them full so they were not hungry!

The ocean is a very dangerous place for baby turtles. They have to be very careful and a bit lucky. There are a lot of fish that like to eat little turtles and big ones. Some of these predators are whales, sharks, eels, and really big fish—scary, huh? Again, that is nature.

Even human beings threaten turtles. Some people eat turtles—some like to keep turtle shells for decoration—it is sad, but true. Some people leave their lights on and confuse the baby turtles. They crawl toward the people-made lights instead of the moonlit path to the sea. Also, sea turtles can get stuck in the nets used by fishing boats.

And, you know, when turtles come to
the surface of the ocean to breathe,
they are sometimes hit by
a boat or a jet ski—OUCH!
Such accidents often injure or
even kill them. It is very, very sad. But, back to the story.

The baby turtles swam and swam away from the shore and toward the
horizon. They were looking for the warm Sargassa Sea and the Sargassum
weed with its little pockets for hiding. Sargassum weed is the perfect
nursery for the sea's tiny critters.
Each baby turtle found a place to hide
and be safe, and a place to find
food for its tummy.

21

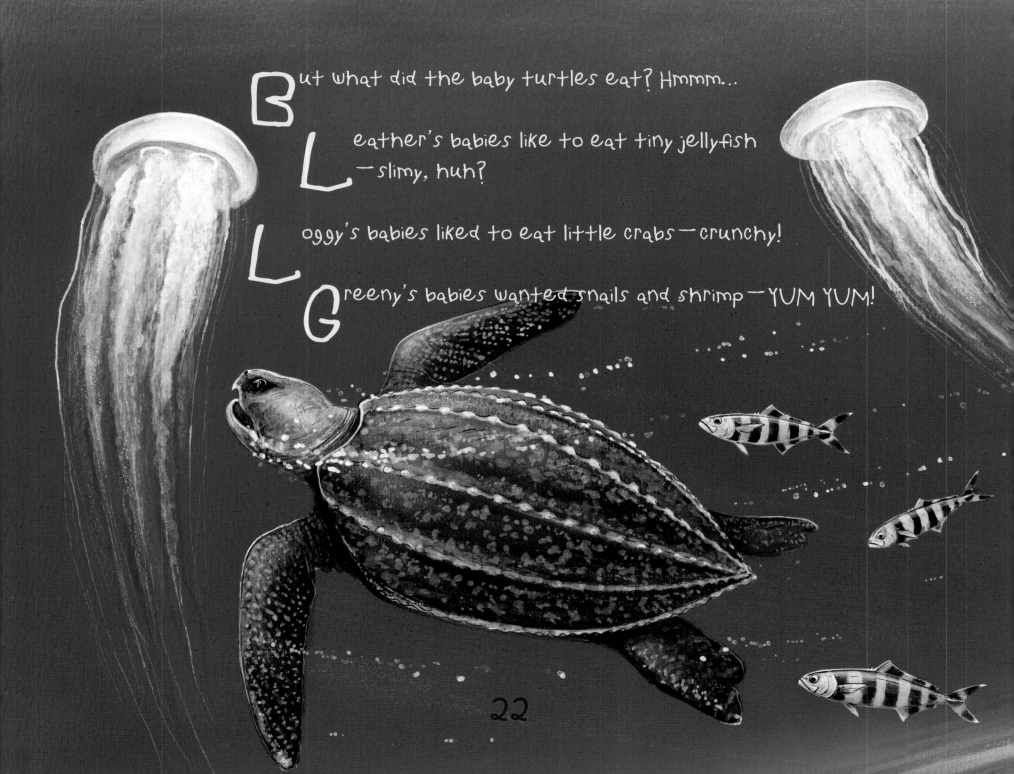

But what did the baby turtles eat? Hmmm...

Leather's babies like to eat tiny jellyfish
—slimy, huh?

Loggy's babies liked to eat little crabs—crunchy!

Greeny's babies wanted snails and shrimp—YUM YUM!

22

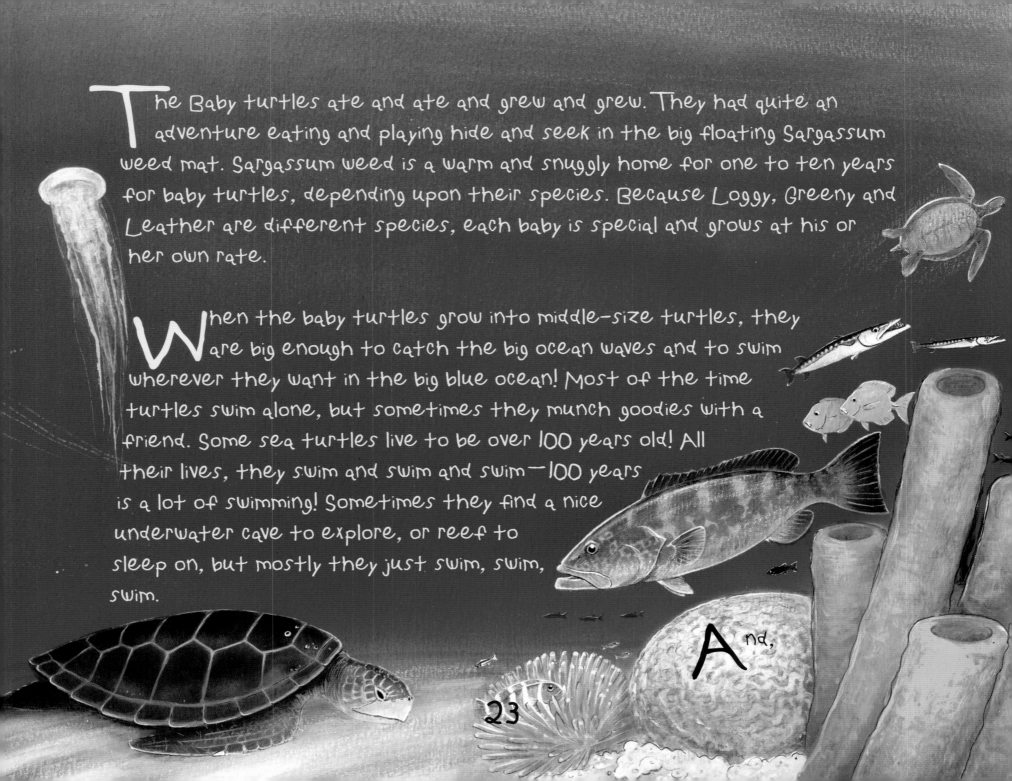

The Baby turtles ate and ate and grew and grew. They had quite an adventure eating and playing hide and seek in the big floating Sargassum weed mat. Sargassum weed is a warm and snuggly home for one to ten years for baby turtles, depending upon their species. Because Loggy, Greeny and Leather are different species, each baby is special and grows at his or her own rate.

When the baby turtles grow into middle-size turtles, they are big enough to catch the big ocean waves and to swim wherever they want in the big blue ocean! Most of the time turtles swim alone, but sometimes they munch goodies with a friend. Some sea turtles live to be over 100 years old! All their lives, they swim and swim and swim—100 years is a lot of swimming! Sometimes they find a nice underwater cave to explore, or reef to sleep on, but mostly they just swim, swim, swim.

And,

23

Did you know that once the baby boy turtles hatch out of their eggs and crawl into the ocean that they never leave the ocean again?

And, do you know that the girl turtles only leave the ocean to lay eggs? And, then they return to their home, the ocean? And, then, you know what?

I'll tell you.

24

Three more female turtles, perhaps even the daughters of Loggy, Greeny and Leather will come back to the same beach where their moms laid their eggs. The daughters will lay their eggs almost in the same spot! Then, the daughters will go back to the ocean.

Again, the moon and sun will watch the eggs until they hatch. The strongest of the baby turtles will survive. It happens over and over again.
    That's nature's way.

That, my friend, is the turtles' way.

THE END. but just the beginning if we do our part!

Note to the Reader

While author Mara Uman Hixon wrote *Turtles' Way: Loggy, Greeny & Leather* for her daughter, the story of sea turtles began approximately two million years ago and is as old as the story of dinosaurs. Dinosaurs became extinct eons ago, yet sea turtles survived. Sadly though, they may soon join the dinosaurs in extinction unless we educate ourselves and our children on how to protect land and sea habitats. The forty miles of the east Florida coastline from Cocoa Beach to Sebastian Inlet, that includes the author's beach house, is one the most important Loggerhead nesting sites in the western hemisphere. During the summer season, the Archie Carr National Wildlife Refuge, Melbourne Beach, averages one sea turtle nest every three feet. Annually, scientists trek to this park to observe and record the nesting and hatching habits of sea turtles.

The same ocean currents that carry the turtles also carry the beach and boat trash that too frequently kills them. Autopsies show that sea critters often mistake floating trash for food. Anything blue, green or grey, or that appears those colors under the water, may be ingested by turtles. Plastic debris is mistaken for jellyfish and rubber of any color is mistaken for plankton. Boat propellers slice; fish hooks snare; and shrimp trawls inadvertently entrap and drown turtles. Fibropapilloma (a deadly virus) is increasingly causing tumors and death in turtles as land run-off pollution increases. Hatchlings are distracted by artifical lights on land. Misled baby turtles seeking the moon-lit path crawl toward beachside lights and become easy prey for raccoons and other predators. As this book goes to press, Loggerheads are listed as a threatened species, Greens are listed as threatened and endangered, and Leatherbacks are endangered. We must do all that we can to assist the survival of sea turtles. We and our children can start by providing pristine nesting beaches, appropriately disposing of all trash, and switching beachfront lights out during nesting season.

The Loggerhead turtle (Caretta caretta) was named for its extremely large log-shaped head. Its powerful jaws crush mollusks, crabs and sea life attached to reefs and rocks. Loggerheads are found in temperate and subtropical coastal waters throughout much of the world and are the sea turtle species most commonly seen close to the USA coasts. Adult Loggerheads feed in the shallow waters along the continental shelves of the Atlantic, Pacific, and Indian oceans. In the Western Hemisphere, they live as far north as Newfoundland and as far south as Argentina. Nesting locations of choice include Florida's east coast barrier islands and Masira Island in Oman. Interestingly, they do not nest on islands in the central and western Pacific. Adult Loggerheads weigh between 200-350 lbs.

The Green turtle (Chelonia mydas) is named for the greenish color of its body fat—it is primarily vegetarian and eats sea grass and seaweed. It has a brownish shell with a starburst pattern on each plate. Greens reach an average weight of 300 lbs and may weigh as much as 500 lbs. Some researchers divide green turtles into two separate species: the Atlantic green and the Pacific green or black. It is a tropical species ranging throughout the warmer areas of the Atlantic, Pacific and Indian Oceans, and in the Mediterranean Sea.

The Leatherback (Dermochelys coriacea) turtles are the largest of all turtles. They dive the deepest and travel the farthest. An adult Leatherback can weigh up to 2000 lbs. They have very long front flippers, but no claws (other sea turtles have at least one claw on each front flipper). Leatherbacks are commonly black with white spots and have long ridges along their smooth rubbery shells (the only turtle without a hard shell). They nest in the tropical Atlantic, Pacific and Indian Oceans. In the Atlantic Ocean, Leatherbacks feed in temperate waters as far north as Canada, Iceland, and Norway. In the Pacific Ocean, they feed as far south as New Zealand and Chile. Eastern Pacific Leatherbacks are much smaller than Atlantic and Indian Ocean Leatherback turtles.

References

Jay, Lorraine A., and McGee, John F., *Sea Turtles* (Our Wild World), NorthWord Press, ISBN 1-559717-46-7, 2000

Maden, Mary, *A Sea Turtle Story*, Dog And Pony Publishing, ISBN 1-890479-63-2, 2000

Orr, Katherine, *Sea Turtles Hatching*, Windward Publising, ISBN 0-893170-48-8, 2002

Ripple, Jeff, *Sea Turtles*, (Worldlife Library), Voyageur Press, ISBN 0-896583-15-5, 1996

Sonnenburg, Maria, *"Sea turtles must cope with the whims of man"*, **Florida Today**, 01 May 2004

Spontila, James R., *Sea Turtles, Complete Guide to Their Biology, Behavior, and Conservation*, John Hopkins University Press, 2004

Van Meter, Victoria B., *"Florida's Sea Turtles"*, **Florida Power and Light**, 1992, revised 2002

Websites:

    Archie Carr National Wildllife Refuge, <archiecarr.fws.gov>

    Fish and Wildlife Research Institute, <floridamarine.org>

    Marathon Turtle Hospital, <turtlehospital.org>

    Monterey Bay Aquarium Research Institute, <mbari.org>

    Monterey Bay National Marine Sanctuary, <mbnms.nos.noaa.gov>

    Sea Turtle Preservation Society, Brevard County, <seaturtlespacecoast.org>

About the Author

Mara Uman Hixon resides in Melbourne Beach, Florida with her husband, Jose; daughter, Isabella; two dogs, Tiger and Princess; and her parrot, Peaches La Rue. Uman Hixon, a former high school science teacher, is the author of *A Rotten Apple*. She is also passionate about art, parenting, animal welfare, the environment, and surfing. After years of observation of sea turtle nesting, she decided to tell the whole turtle story to Isabella, so that she and children everywhere may learn to love the complexities and nuances of nature.

About the Artist

Originally from Stuart, Florida, Steve J. Harris has always lived on the water and made the ocean his second home. Accomplished as an artist at an early age, and as an avid surfer and sport fisherman, Harris captures the allure of the sea making it one of his trademarks. After graduating from Fort Lauderdale Art Institute with a degree in Commercial Art, Harris worked in South Florida in advertising and graphic illustration, winning awards and industry recognition. His work graces homes, hotels, and restaurants in the area. In fall 1996, Harris moved to Cocoa Beach, Florida, where he focuses on fine art, working in several mediums and styles. His work can be seen at *<stevejharrisart.com>*.